Love Me Later

Julie Baer

FIRST EDITION, 2005
1 2 3 4 5 6 7 8 9 10

The illustrations were made with cut-paper collage, using found material.
Monarch butterflies were painted in gouache on rice paper, borders in acrylic on rice paper.
Typeset in Ike Regular and Optima on an Apple Macintosh computer.

Book design by Julie Baer and Shawn Towne

Library of Congress Cataloging-in-Publication Data

Baer, Julie.
Love me later / by Julie Baer.-- 1st ed.
    p. cm.
    Summary: One afternoon in his backyard, amidst butterflies, squirrels, and
other creatures, young Abe asks his parents about what he did when he was
little, while avoiding the hugs and kisses their memories provoke.
    ISBN 1-932188-03-7 (alk. paper)
[1. Parent and child--Fiction. 2. Growth--Fiction. 3. Jews--United
States--Fiction. 4. Monarch butterfly--Fiction. 5. Butterflies--Fiction.
6. Urban ecology (Biology)--Fiction.] I. Title.

PZ7.B1397Lo 2004
[E]--dc22

2003022951

Thank you forever, Staley and Mike Krause. Thanks, Sawyer and Collin, for sharing. Many thanks also to Peter Sis,
Rob Shepperson, Howard Schwartz, Robin Chase, Maria Lockheardt, Jim McDonald of The Art Connection,
Shawn Towne, Lori Plaut, Paul and Rich Lam of Pictex, Ma Yan of Imago, Tino Kwok of Bright Arts, Caren Loebel-Fried,
Dilys Evans, Andy Ferren of Goulston & Storrs, Marc and Darlene Miller, Norah Dooley, Nancy and Jim Farley of
Farley's Bookshop, Linda Silver, Kenny and Chuck Vorspan, Richard and Phyllis Kluger, Karen Kosko, Todd McKie,
Keith Warren, David and Joanne Baer, Bette Baer, Harriet Schwartz, and Efrain Mora.

BOLLiX
books

A butterfly is sitting on my nose!

It just flew down and landed there, I mean HERE. It tickles! "Ma!" I yell. But the butterfly flies away. I watch it flutter around the little maple tree and the street light and the telephone pole, and then across the street toward my friend Justin's house.

"Ma! A butterfly was on my nose!"
I jump up into the air. I'm flying!

"A butterfly? On your nose? Maybe it was tired. Or hungry, and found some leftovers from lunch."

"Ma, when I was little what did I want to be when I grew up? An astronaut? A deep sea diver? An explorer?"

"Oh, lots of things. One time you said, 'Ma, when I grow up I want to be an artist just like you and draw pictures just like the ones you draw. We'll do it together, Ok? And I'll sit on your lap!' I told you, Abe, when you grow up you'll be bigger than I am, so I'll have to sit on YOUR lap!"

She is smiling at me in a way that looks like she wants to kiss me. Uh oh. No good. "Love me later," I say, and I run away, through the pigeons, around the little maple tree, and up to our front door.

I reach out and touch the little box inside the doorway, and then I kiss my fingers, because it's a mezuzah, and inside is real Hebrew writing reminding my house that it's a special place.

Inside the house, I look around the kitchen and pick a banana, a greenish one. It's dark and cool in here. I stand by the window and watch the cats swishing their tails and twitching their ears. Outside, a squirrel is staring in at them, and its tail is flashing and swishing too. It's funny that the cats are watching the squirrel and the squirrel is watching the cats, and I'm watching them! I wonder if tail-flashing is a way of talking. I pretend I'm flashing my own tail, throw away the banana peel, and go back outside.

LOOK

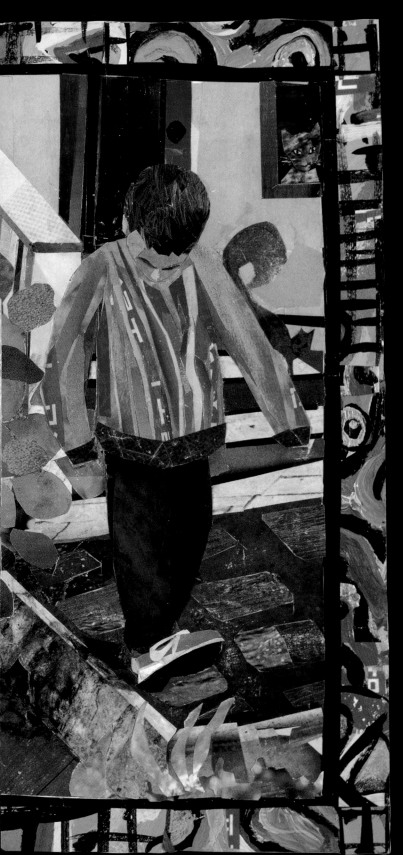

It's bright out here. I hope I left some banana on my nose for the butterfly, because I hope it comes back. This time I'll remember not to yell "Ma!"

"Oh no! MA! Ma! I'm sorry to say that I just killed an ant."

My mom is sitting in the grass, drawing. She looks up at me, frowning a little.

"Ma, did I ever invent anything?"

She squints her eyes.

"Oh, yeah, I remember. You made up a word.
Punkyum. You claimed it was a Hebrew word.
And you had all the kids in your preschool
running around like loonies, yelling, 'Punkyum!
Punkyum!' I don't think it really is Hebrew,
but I could be wrong."

"LOOK, there's a daddy long legs.

What other things did I do?"

"Wow, such long legs! Ok, here's a story about baby Abe: One night you cried for hours. We offered you a bottle, rocked you, sang to you, but you just cried and cried and cried."

"Why was I crying?"   "Good question!"

"So, still crying, you crawled across Dad and reached for the glass of water on his nightstand. He gave you a sip but you kept on crying and crying.

Then you picked up Dad's glasses, sat up, and put them on. And then you laughed! You did that for about ten minutes: taking off the glasses, putting them back on, and laughing. And then you went to sleep."

"Ma, those little brown birds keep calling me 'cheap, cheap, cheap!'"

She looks at me, kind of smiling, and then says, "Come here, Fred." Oh no, when she starts Fredding me, it means she's about to hug me. I'm out of here. Plus, here are Dewey and Dad just coming in the gate.

"Love me later, Ma," I say, and I follow Dad and Dewey into the house. I remember to kiss the mezuzah on the way in.

FRED

"Dad, what did I do when I was little?" I pull off my sweatshirt. Dad is making dinner. Rice and beans, my favorite. I see a bowl of orange cheese and take a handful.

"Let me see, Abe." Dad is chopping onions. "Well, you invented this fantastic word that you claimed was Hebrew – "

"I know: punkyum. What does it mean?"

"You're asking ME? Ok, I remember this: every day as we were driving Dewey to his old school and you to Irene and Nick's daycare, we would pass the public library and the City Hall, both big, memorable buildings. We had spent some time in the library, so you knew its name. As we passed it, you would yell out, 'Libe-way!' And then the City Hall, 'Hallway!'"

"No way!"

Now Dad is smiling at me in that way! Uh oh.

"Later, Dad, later," I say.

I go over and open the door for my mom, who comes inside, holding the picture she drew. I kiss the mezuzah for her, because I like to.

family

friend

"Abe, I remembered a good story for you, about the first time Jess came to baby-sit."

"OUR Jess?" I ask.

"Yes, our Jess. She was only a teenager. You were little - only two or three. The doorbell rang while Daddy and I were still upstairs getting dressed to go out. I hurried down the stairs just as you were opening the door, and I heard you say, 'Hi, my name is Abe and my daddy's upstairs pooping.'"

"I said that? And Jess was a stranger?"

"Yes, well, you had some information to
relate, right? Well, Dewey came in, and
we showed Jess around, and I began filling
her in on bedtimes and emergency numbers.
Soon Daddy came downstairs and introduced
himself to Jess and said, 'Hi, I'm Abe's dad,
and, just for the record, I was shaving.'"

"He wasn't pooping?
        Ma, now can I see your picture?

Hey! My butterfly! It came back!"

trust

Dad is walking by with a bottle of hot sauce. He stops and looks at my butterfly and smiles, and then he gives Mom a hug. So I wrap my arms around them too - because Mom drew my butterfly, and because Dad made rice and beans, my favorite.

And because later is now.

Can you find 10 monarch butterflies, 1 grasshopper, 2 monarch caterpillars, 1 ant,
7 ox-eye daisies, 1 cardinal, 2 ladybird beetles, 2 daddy long legs, 2 bears, 7 pigeons,
4 green Japanese maple branches, 1 tiger swallowtail butterfly, 6 marsh pink flowers, 3 crows,
1 sparrow, 1 feather, 1 catbird, 2 red maple leaves, 2 spiders, 8 pictures of Abe's inside cats,
1 outside cat, 3 squirrels, 1 chickadee, and 1 yellow heartleaf arnica flower?

Imagine millions of monarch butterflies flying from Canada and the United States all the way to forests in
the mountains of Mexico! It happens every year. It's amazing! Almost as amazing as a butterfly sitting on
your nose. But these mountain forests, where the monarchs go to rest each winter, are being cut down.
After their rest, the monarchs return north to eat and breed, but fields of the milkweed and nectar plants
they need are being converted into lawns and parking lots. Many people love monarch butterflies and
want to help them. You can help them! You can make your community a better home for monarchs by
planting and preserving their milkweed plants and flowers, even in your own backyard! You can help
make sure more trees are planted in the monarchs' wintertime homes in Mexico. Here are some people
you can contact to learn more and help:

Journey North
www.learner.org/jnorth
Engaging students in a global
study of wildlife migration
and seasonal change

Monarch Butterfly Sanctuary Foundation
www.mlmp.org
Preserving the Mexican
overwintering sites through research,
economic support and education

Monarchs in the Classroom
www.monarchlab.org
Instructional materials and
research opportunities for
K-12 educators and parents

Michoacan Reforestation Fund
www.michoacanmonarchs.org
Helping people and other
creatures by conserving the
forests they live in